THE TREMBLING TOWER

ALEXANDRIA BLAELOCK

Also by Alexandria Blaelock

MS BLAELOCK'S BOOKS
Stress Free Dinner Parties
Signature Wardrobe Planning
Holistic Personal Finance
Minimally Viable Housekeeping
Planning a Life Worth Living

FICTION
That Love Nonsense
Taipan vs Brown
The Ghost and Ms Cox
Friends Like That
Weaving the Wildwood

SHORT STORY COLLECTIONS
The Histories of Hayward Hall
Lovelorn, Lovestruck and Love at First Sight
Common or Garden Variety Heroes
Case Files of the Wilkinson Detective Agency
Unavoidable Fates
Christmas Travesties
Five Faces of Felicia Clarke
Little Place Called Home
Security Directorate Dossiers vol 1.
Security Directorate Dossiers vol 2.

A SELECTION OF AVAILABLE SHORT STORIES

Alma's Grace	Pursuit of Power
Bygone Boyfriend	Ship in a Bottle
Cracking the COde	Susan and the Gangster
Dwennon's Despair	The Cookie Shop
Fate in Your Hands	The Pseudonym's Bride
Needy Bitch	Waylon's Way

THE TREMBLING TOWER

ALEXANDRIA BLAELOCK

BlueMere Books
MELBOURNE, AUSTRALIA

For permission requests, please contact
enquiries@bluemerebooks.com.

Ordering Information:
Discounts are available on quantity purchases. For details, contact orders@bluemerebooks.com.

The Trembling Tower/Alexandria Blaelock
paperback ISBN: 9781923083035
digital ISBN: 9781923083042

Book Layout © BookDesignTemplates.com
Cover Art © Spanychev/Depositphotos

THE TREMBLING TOWER

The Edwardian apartment building, quite simply, was delightful.

The white painted woodwork was daintily opulent in contrast to the warm and welcoming golden-brown bricks. Its elegant arched windows, the chic round corner towers, and charming stained-glass door set lent it an air of fairy tale enchantment.

It wasn't hard to imagine a bunch of fairy tale princesses sharing the rooftop flat.

Sleeping Beauty taking long Saturday afternoon naps on the couch while the Little Mermaid hogged the Bathroom, and Rapunzel combed her hair out the lounge room window.

Maybe, after a late night out on the town, Cinderella would cook a mammoth hangover-curing full English breakfast while Beauty took her chihuahua for a run in the local park.

Just standing on the downhill side of the street from it made Helene King smile.

She almost didn't care what the vacant apartment looked like. It was hard enough to find an inner-city apartment, let alone one in her price range. So tempting to just take it just on the basis of its façade, location, and ridiculously cheap rent.

It was so much more inviting than its square, dark and squat Victorian neighbour.

But.

There's no point sending good money after bad - she was here because;

a) her current lease had expired, and

b) she was sick of flat sharing, and

c) she needed to economise.

The building was a handy five-minute stroll from the train station and a supermarket. And if she had to economise further, it was just a brisk 45-minute walk to work.

She'd probably get faster as she got used it too.

And if the flat was wind and watertight, neat and clean, not even ghosts or fairy tale monsters would stop her from taking it.

Though the amount of neat and clean was negotiable.

As was wind and watertight.

And really, a few monsters about the place would stop her getting too lonely at night.

She pulled the key from her sky-blue wool coat pocket as she crossed the road.

It fit snugly in the lock and turned without unnecessarily jiggling.

A good sign.

Coloured sunshine poured through the stained-glass windows and over the immaculate black and white foyer tiles. The room was warm, but not too hot as the transom above the door was open a wee crack. The doormat was clean, and the mail neatly filed in the boxes.

By the little people presumably.

As she climbed the three flights of stairs, the carpet was clean, though coloured by light spilling from a set of matching stained-glass windows in the street frontage. The smooth white walls, were a little scuffed and marked, though overall it looked more like graduations of colour than grime.

No cracks or large chips, no obvious signs of structural concerns.

So far, the place was pretty, if a little tired. But the building was almost four times Helene's age, so not looking too bad for an old girl.

And at the pinnacle, the crisp blue door of the apartment she'd come to inspect.

The air was clean and fresh, no hint of damp, leftover curry, or cigarette smoke.

What could possibly be wrong with the place that the rent was so cheap?

Were the monsters real even if the princesses weren't?

Helene steeled herself as she punched in the temporary security code.

The door lock chirped cheerfully as it popped open and a bright, odourless beam of daylight escaped into the corridor.

The flat was cleaner than she'd expected. Freshly painted, going by the small specks of pale blue paint on the carpet. It seemed quite spacious, but the complete lack of furniture probably accounted for that.

The kitchen was immaculate, with barely any baked-on grease in the oven. Clean windows, trimmed with a faded country rose print blind, framed a mysterious view of imaginary cockney chimney sweeps dancing across neighbouring rooftops and through their gardens.

The fridge door was chocked open with a matching teacup.

If there were any cockroaches in there, odds on they tied their feelers back with tiny ribbons and capered about the place in stilettos.

The adjoining lounge/dining room might not be quite large enough for both activities simultaneously, but the kitchen counter made a sort of breakfast bar. And while you stood in the kitchen, waiting for the coffee maker to finish, you could look across it and through your own arched window down the street.

Or watching for your boyfriend to turn up.

Anyway, who really sits down to eat at home these days?

People who eat instant noodles, that's who.

And you can eat those out of the pot while you're sitting cross-legged on the couch in your fluffy bunny pyjamas while watching the latest episode of some gritty crime drama on free to air television.

Maybe while you're sharing a cheap Beaujolais with your new neighbours, the princesses.

The tiny bathroom had a big old, white, enamelled claw-foot tub. A separate shower would have been nice, but climbing into the bath for a shower was the usual. And who doesn't, now and again, like to lie in the tub with warm water raining down on them?

The back half of the flat was taken up with a bedroom and a dressing room.

Or a study.

Or if you were minimalists, two bedrooms.

Helene pulled aside the plush red velvet curtains of what she thought was the "Master" and looked out over the streets behind the building. She could see a tunnel, but not whether it was road, rail, or maybe canal. But right on top of it, a sweet little hobby farm with a couple of horses and a goat.

And some other creature she couldn't identify.

Maybe a pig.

That'd be the McDonald's farm she thought snorting.

The fairy tale flat was adorable! It was inconceivable anyone could live in it and not be utterly happy.

Maybe she was rash, and a little foolish, but shopping for a new home was exhausting and expensive, and she only had a fortnight left to get out of the place she was living right now.

This flat was the first decent place she'd seen since she started looking what seemed a lifetime ago.

Helene decided she couldn't let it go.

Especially as it was Friday, she could shop and move in over the weekend, and not need to take any time off work.

Her boss, the secretary eating ghoul, would like that.

She pulled out her phone and took a few pics, then rushed back to the agent to sign the contract and pay the deposit and first month's rent.

And because it was so cheap, she had a few hundred dollars left over to buy furniture and bits and pieces she'd need to move in with.

She couldn't wait!

And as she checked her watch, she realised she *really* couldn't wait and ran, coat and hair streaming behind her for the station. Now that she'd rent to pay, she really needed to get back to the office before the ghoul got back from his lunch.

Even though that meant she had to settle for buying an egg salad sandwich because no one ate them by choice and that made them the quickest lunch she could get.

And when the inevitable gaseous disturbances hit, it would serve him right.

《《 • 》》

Once the workday was over, and her boss had finally left, Helene just wanted to go home.

Her new home that is, not the shitty place she'd been sharing with strangers.

She wished she could just get on the train and go there to find her fairy godmother had waved her magic wand, and it was warm and welcoming, and most importantly, comfortably furnished with overstuffed couches and threadbare Turkish rugs.

A quick train ride got her to the shopping district, and she ate a few warm hand-held snacks in between ducking in and out of discount stores for quilts, pillows, towels, and scented candles before catching the train back to the new place.

Awkward, but not insurmountable to carry home bulk shopping.

Though next time, she'd probably get a cab.

Or home delivery.

And as she struggled down the street from the station, shifting her shopping from aching hand to aching hand, she took the time to survey her new neighbourhood.

The supermarket. A pub.

She ducked into the pub and bought a bottle of cheap champagne.

News agency, hairdresser, travel agent, curry house.

Another pub.

Café.

Fish and chip shop, kebab shop, dumpling house.

All the necessities of life.

Plus, a charity shop and a second-hand shop. Wait, had they been there that morning? Would they still be there tomorrow?

She struggled up the stairs and through her front door, pushing her shoes off with her toes before staggering into the lounge to dump her shopping in the middle of the room.

Then she hung her coat on a peg next to the door, turned the fridge on, rinsed out the teacup then filled it with champagne.

Taking a moment, Helene closed her eyes and listened to the expectant silence in the flat. Almost as if it was holding its breath, though whether that was to scream in horror or shout welcome wasn't yet clear.

What was clear, was even empty, the flat felt comfortable and homely. Like putting on warm snuggly pyjamas after being caught in a winter storm. As if all her cares and worries were a just smear on the doormat outside.

She raised her cup to the flat, "your good health," she toasted. And it seemed a little like the flat let its breath out and relaxed.

She carried her champagne to the arched window, opened it and sat on the windowsill, the carpet pleasantly scratchy against her bare feet.

She took a sip as she watched the people in the street. Blokes in the pub on the corner's beer garden chanted football songs, and the roar from nearby apartments watching the match on TV suggested someone'd scored. The brittle laughter of bored, drunk girlfriends pierced the clamour.

The lights of the city laid out below her rivalled the stars up above, and it seemed the darkness sparkled with magic.

A light, cool, curry scented breeze blew through the window.

She drained the cup and set it on the floor, then rifled through the shopping bags until she found a quilt, then wrapped it around herself.

She leant her arm on the sill, and her head in the crook of her elbow and watched some more.

And as the excitement of the day caught up with her, her eyes closed, and she drifted off to sleep. And as her sleep deepened, it seemed the flat was rocking her gently to sleep.

The next day, she woke too early, cramped, and a little hungover.

Her wonderful new home was flooded with slightly too much bright sunshine and too little coffee.

The stroll through the fresh air and sunshine to the café restored a little of her humanity, and a decent fry up the rest.

Over her second coffee, she thought about the bare minimum she'd need to be comfortable in the short term.

Something to sleep on.

Something to cook with.

Something to eat and drink from.

Something to eat and drink.

Something to sleep on would have to be new because eewwww.

And it would have to be delivered, and if she did that first, maybe the fairy godmother she didn't have could make sure it was delivered today.

And in between, she'd go back to the old place and pack her things, which wouldn't take too long.

On her way to the station, on a whim, she dropped into the second-hand store and found a couple of lovely old pieces of furniture to buy later if no one else got in first.

Plus, a futon, wrapped in plastic. The store owner explained it was new, ordered by a couple who'd broken up shortly before it was delivered.

And the delivery truck was moving out as soon as they finished loading it. And as the futon was relatively small and light, if she wanted it today, they could fit it in the truck and deliver it in about an hour.

Perfect.

That was half the job done, and she hadn't even left home.

So to speak.

She crossed the road to the charity shop and got a load of stuff for cooking, eating, and drinking with, so that was pretty much all the basics sorted and the day wasn't even half over.

Helene wondered if perhaps she did have a fairy godmother, but one who preferred to operate discreetly behind the scenes rather than wands blazing, out in the open.

The rest of the day passed in a blur of train and bus rides to pack up at her old flat, and to buy food and cleaning supplies for the new place.

By the time the sun set in a flush of purple and orange, she was exhausted.

The lounge room was haphazardly stacked with boxes and bags of old and new belongings while she lay in the bath with a warm mineral soak, a book, and a glass of wine.

She looked forward to sleeping on the new futon, currently airing out by the arched window, and ignoring the need to unpack and wash the other things.

Now that she was more or less settled, there was plenty of time.

Wiggling her toes and sending small waves back and forward in the tub, she idly thought about televisions, clothes washers, and other appliances to start saving up for.

The first movement of the building was almost imperceptible against the already tidal bathwater.

Then, Helene heard glasses gently clinking, as if someone was carrying them unsteadily on a tray.

Which was impossible given she was alone in the flat.

She sat up in the bath, clutching its edges and tilting her head to listen as the clinking got louder, the tremors more noticeable, and the ripples in the tub deep enough to slosh over the edge.

Her heart skipped a beat or two as she slithered out of the bath, grabbed a towel, and wrapped it about herself as she crawled into the hallway and crouched next to the wall. But almost as soon as she was more or less secure, the tremors eased, and it was almost as if nothing had happened.

Aside from her still racing heart.

She stumbled into the lounge and threw on the first clothes she saw.

Then ran around the flat checking for internal damage, and looking out the windows found nothing, inside or out.

She ran down the stairs, two at a time, but didn't see any people evacuating or congregating on the street, though it was late Saturday night.

The building exterior was undamaged, no one seemed concerned, so she retraced her steps back into the flat.

An earthquake was such a weird flukish event to end the day with, and without a TV or radio, she was forced to check the Internet to find out more.

But there was nothing to find.

She waited a few minutes, dancing with impatience, then checked again.

Still nothing.

How odd.

And very inconvenient should she find out she had to move out after just moving in.

Though at least she didn't have money invested in the place.

She decided no news was good news, and it was probably safe to sleep in the flat.

But she was reluctant to move out of the relative safety of the lounge, so she flopped the futon on the floor, covered it with a quilt and threw a pillow on the top.

Despite her concern, she slept deeply and woke refreshed to a new, but rainy day.

It didn't take long to sort out, wash up and put away her stuff. And by the time she was done, she had a new list of things to buy and the time to shop for them.

It was late by the time she got home. A little too late to eat out, so she picked up dumplings on her way.

Helene was climbing the stairs when the building started to shake, and while she didn't think it was safe outside, she thought it was less safe on the stairs, so she scuttled back outside.

Eyes squeezed shut tight, clutching her shopping, and trying not to let her imagination carry away with her, she was surprised when someone brushed past her on their way into the building.

Scared as she was, she didn't think she could let them go without warning, so she gave chase, calling "hello, excuse me, it's not safe to enter a building during an earthquake."

She was surprised by a burst of feminine laughter from the stairs above her.

"What time is it?"

Helene looked at her watch, "it's ten past ten, though I don't see—"

"It isn't an earthquake.

"This building is located on the convergence of two overground train lines and one underground. Every night, at this time, there's a train on all three tracks, and it shakes the building."

"Is it safe?"

"Yes Hen, it is. The tracks were here before the building, and that's been here more than a century. It just takes a little getting used to that's all."

"That's a relief, I just moved in."

"Oh, are you new in apartment six?"

"Yes, I am."

"How wonderful," the steps came down the stairs again, and a beautiful young woman who looked a lot like a fairy tale princess said, "I'm Elissa, I'm across the hall from you. Can I give you a hand with your shopping?"

"I'd love that," said Helene as she followed her new friend home.

THE END

ABOUT THE AUTHOR

Alexandria Blaelock writes stories, some of them for *Ellery Queen's Mystery Magazine* and *Pulphouse Fiction Magazine.*

She's also written five self-help books applying business techniques to personal matters like getting dressed, cleaning house, and feeding your friends.

She lives in a forest because she enjoys birdsong, and the smell of gum leaves. When not telecommuting to parallel universes from her Melbourne based imagination, she watches K-dramas, talks to animals, and drinks Campari. At the same time.

Discover more at alexandriablaelock.com.

IF YOU ENJOYED THIS STORY...

Why not try *Little Place Called Home*

Home is where the heart is.
You can struggle to find the place you call home. It's not a place, it's a feeling. You'll know it when you find it.
This collection of short stories explores our search for a place we can call home.

- In Cry in the Darkness, Tom struggles to find his place taming a grant of land.
- While Millie and the Mountain shows sometimes the place finds you.
- As Mrs Pearson discovers in Dream House, letting it go can be harder than you expect.
- Meanwhile, in Dingo Hunting, Katie finds her place when she finds a new family.
- And in Dance of Death, Li Quan finds his place in the afterlife changes according to where his heart is.

Short, sweet and relatable, these stories will make you homesick for places you've never been.